Nate the Great
and the
Boring Beach Bag

Nate the Great
and the
Boring Beach Bag

by Marjorie Weinman Sharmat
illustrated by Marc Simont

A YEARLING BOOK

Text copyright © 1987 by Marjorie Weinman Sharmat
Cover and interior illustrations copyright © 1987 by Marc Simont
Extra Fun Activities text copyright © 2005 by Emily Costello
Extra Fun Activities illustrations copyright © 2005 by Jody Wheeler

All rights reserved. Published in the United States by Yearling, an imprint of
Random House Children's Books, a division of Penguin Random House LLC,
New York. Originally published in paperback in the United States by Delacorte
Press, an imprint of Random House Children's Books, New York, in 1987.
Reprinted by arrangement with the Putnam and Grosset Group.

Yearling and the jumping horse design are registered trademarks of
Penguin Random House LLC.

Visit us on the Web! randomhousekids.com
Educators and librarians, for a variety of teaching tools, visit us at
RHTeachersLibrarians.com

Library of Congress Cataloging-in-Publication Data is available upon request.
ISBN 978-0-440-40168-1 (pbk.) — ISBN 978-0-385-37675-4 (ebook)

Printed in the United States of America
62 61 60 59 58
First Yearling Edition 1989

To the beach of my childhood,
Old Orchard Beach, Maine

I, Nate, the great detective,
was swimming in the ocean
with my dog, Sludge.

Someone was swimming behind us.

It was Oliver.

Oliver is always behind me.

Oliver is a pest.

He swam up beside me.

"I lost my seashell,"

he said. "I want you to find it."

"I, Nate the Great,

do not look for seashells.

If I did, I could find plenty
of them on this beach."
"The seashell was in my beach bag,"
Oliver said. "But that is gone, too."
"Your beach bag is gone?"
"Yes," Oliver said. "My clothes
and shoes were in it."
"Your clothes and shoes, too?
You need clothes.
You need shoes.
You need me.

I, Nate the Great,
will take your case."
Sludge, Oliver, and I swam to shore.
We sat down on the sand.

I took a pencil and a piece of paper

out of my swimsuit pocket.

I wrote a note to my mother.

It was soggy and sandy.

I hoped she could read it.

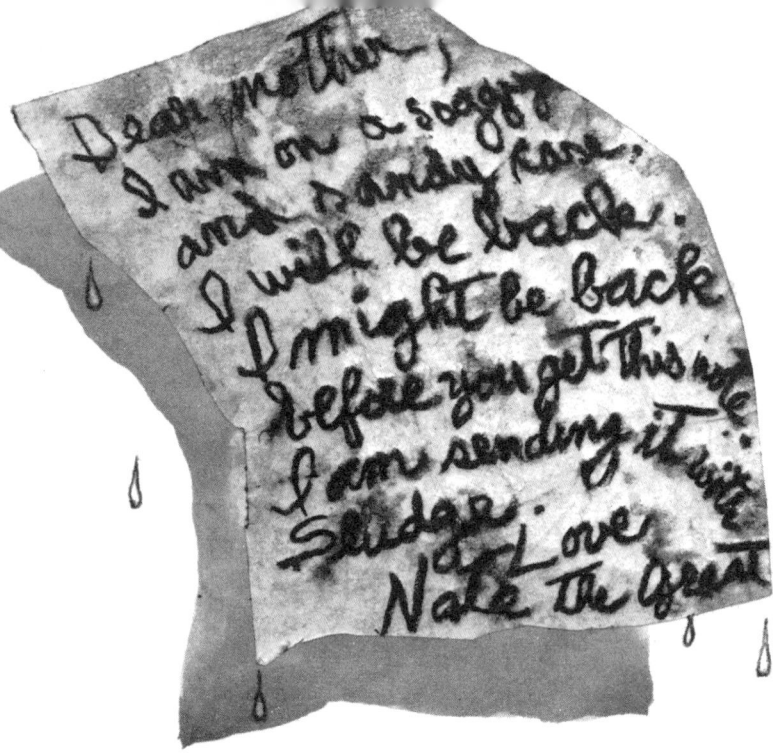

Dear mother,
I am on a soggy
and sandy case.
I will be back.
I might be back
before you get this note.
I am sending it with
Sludge.
Love
Nate the Great

I put the note in Sludge's mouth.
"Take this home
and then come back," I said.
"Don't stop to eat
along the way."
Sludge ran off with the note.
I hoped he would be back soon.

I hoped he would be back.

Oliver and I walked along the beach.

"Show me where you last saw
your beach bag," I said.

"I left it on the beach,"
Oliver said, "while I bought
a glass of water
at Rosamond's Restaurant."

"Rosamond has a restaurant?"

"Yes. She is selling water,
seaweed soup, and sandwiches.
The sandwiches are filled with sand.
She said that
since they are called sandwiches,
they should be made of sand."

"It figures," I said.

Oliver stopped.

"When I got back
to where I left my beach bag,
it was gone. And here is where
I left it."

"How do you know that?" I asked.

"Because I left my beach ball

14

beside it. And see, my beach ball
is still here. Nobody took it."
"If someone took your beach bag,
why would they leave your beach ball?"
I asked. "Was there something special
about your beach bag?
What did it look like?"
"It was blue.
It was blank.
It was boring,"
Oliver said.
"And it was bumpy
from all the stuff inside it."
I, Nate the Great, looked down
at the beach ball
and the sand around it.

"The sand is not pressed down
where your beach bag was," I said,
"even though the bag was heavy
with clothes, shoes,
and a shell inside it."
"Is that a clue?" Oliver asked.
"It may be an important clue
or no clue at all," I said.
"Sand gets kicked around.
Tell me, were you alone when
you left your beach bag here?"

"I was sitting all by myself,"
Oliver said. "Then I saw
Annie and her dog, Fang,
running toward me.
Whenever I see Fang
running toward me,
I run, too.
I run away.
I ran to Rosamond's Restaurant."
"We will have to walk to
Rosamond's Restaurant," I said.

"We will look for clues
and your boring beach bag
along the way."
Oliver and I started to walk.
The sun felt hot
on my back.

The sand felt scratchy
between my toes.
I was careful not to step
on sand castles
or ice cream sticks.
I ducked beach balls in the air.

I looked for Oliver's beach bag.

I also looked for Sludge.

He should have been back by now.

We passed a refreshment stand.

I wondered if they served pancakes.

I wanted to stop.

But I had a case to solve.

I saw Rosamond up ahead.

She was sitting behind a crate.

Sometimes people get strange

sitting under a hot sun.

But Rosamond is strange all the time.

Rosamond's four cats were asleep

on the crate.

Oliver and I walked up to her.

"Have you seen Oliver's

boring beach bag?" I asked.

"No," Rosamond said. "I have been
too busy with my restaurant.
Want to buy a sandwich or soup
or a glass of water?"
"No. I must find the beach bag.
Oliver has no clothes, no shoes,
and no seashell."
"Oh, dear," Rosamond said.
"I will give him some free water.
And part of a sandwich."
Rosamond handed Oliver
a glass of sandy water.
I knew it was time to leave.
Oliver and I started to walk back
to where he said he had left
his beach bag.

"I did not find your beach bag
between where you left it
and Rosamond's Restaurant," I said.
"I also did not find my dog."
I, Nate the Great, was thinking.
Sludge must have stopped somewhere
to eat.
That sounded like a good idea.
"I am going to stop
at the refreshment stand," I said.
I walked up to the refreshment stand.
Oliver followed me.
Then he stopped.
Suddenly I knew why.
Annie's dog, Fang, was tied
to a post beside the stand.

His teeth gleamed

under the bright sun.

He looked hungry.

He looked at me.

I did not want to stay.

But Annie was there.

Perhaps she had seen Oliver's bag.

I talked fast.

"I am looking for Oliver's

beach bag," I said.

"It looks boring.

Have you seen it?"

"Yes, it was beside
a beach ball," Annie said.
"Fang and I ran by it,
just as Oliver ran off.
Fang and I are running
from one end of the beach
to the other.

I stopped for a snack.

But Fang is trying to lose weight.

He is on a diet."

"He is eating the post

you tied him to," I said.

"But that is not on his diet!"

Annie cried.

She rushed to Fang

and untied him.

"Is a beach bag on his diet?"

I asked.

"Not today," Annie said.

Annie and Fang ran off.

They ran in the opposite direction

from Rosamond's Restaurant.

Fang was not so hungry

that he would eat a sandwich

made of sand.

I, Nate the Great, was hungry.

I ate some pancakes

at the refreshment stand

and thought about the case.

There was not much to think about.

I did not have one clue

that I knew was a clue.

I also did not have a dog.

Where was Sludge?

Suddenly I saw him on the beach.

He was with Oliver.

I finished my pancakes fast.

I went up to Sludge and Oliver.

Sludge was still holding my note

in his mouth.

He looked hot and tired.

"You were supposed to take
that note home," I said.
Perhaps Sludge did not know
where home was.
The beach looks the same
for miles and miles.
Sand and water.
All that sand
and all that water

must have mixed him up.

Sludge sat down and rested.

Oliver and I sat with him.

Then Sludge ran into the water
to cool off.

The *water*.

I had been looking for Oliver's
beach bag on land.

But what if it was in the water?

I ran into the water.

I swam here.

I swam there.

I looked and looked
for Oliver's beach bag.

All of a sudden I saw it!

It was bobbing in the water
up ahead.

A bump.

A big blue bump.

Sludge and I swam up to it.

I grabbed it.

It was not Oliver's beach bag.

It was Esmeralda's head.

"What are you doing?" she asked.

"I am looking for Oliver's

beach bag," I said.

"Oliver!" cried Esmeralda.

"I am hiding from him.

He follows me everywhere.

On land.

On sea.

And here he comes!"

Esmeralda swam away.

Oliver swam up.

"Did you find my beach bag?"
he asked.

"Not yet," I said.

"I will follow you
until you solve the case,"
Oliver said.

"And even after I solve the case,"
I said.

Sludge and I swam to shore.

Oliver swam to shore.

Sludge and I stretched out

on the sand.

Oliver stretched out

on the sand behind us.

He had given me a tough case.

Nobody had given me any clues.

Or had they?

There was no dent in the sand

from Oliver's beach bag.

What if it meant something?

What if it meant that

Oliver's beach bag

had *never* been there?

But Oliver said it had.

What else did he say?

He said that Annie and Fang

were running toward him

just before he left

his beach bag and beach ball

and ran to Rosamond's Restaurant.

I, Nate the Great, got a stick.

I smoothed out some sand.

Then I drew a map in it.

I marked where Oliver's beach ball was.

I marked Rosamond's Restaurant.

I marked the refreshment stand,

which was between them.

I had seen Annie and Fang

at the refreshment stand.

Annie said that they were running

from one end of the beach

to the other.

She said they had run past
Oliver's beach bag and ball.
I looked at my map.
First there was the beach ball.
Then the refreshment stand.
Then Rosamond's Restaurant.
When Annie and Fang left
the refreshment stand,
they should have run
toward Rosamond's Restaurant.
But they ran in the opposite direction.
Why?
I, Nate the Great, was stumped.
I looked at Sludge.
Sludge always helps with my cases.
But all the sand and water

had mixed him up this time.

Did Annie and Fang get mixed up?

No. Annie would not

get mixed up.

I looked at Oliver.

It would be easy

for him to get mixed up.

He was always following someone.

I kicked some sand.

I ducked a beach ball.

I thought.

Hmm.

"Oliver," I said.

"I think I know

where your beach bag is.

Follow me."

"Of course," Oliver said.

Sludge and I walked
to Rosamond's Restaurant.
We walked *past* Rosamond's Restaurant.
"Wait!" Oliver said.
"You are going very far away
from where I left my beach bag."
I, Nate the Great, kept on walking.
Up ahead I saw something in the sand.

ROSAMOND'S RESTAURANT
COLD WATER 3¢ A GLASS
SEAWEED SOUP A PICKLE
SANDWICHES ALL SAND
NO FAKE 4 CENTS

I ran up to it.

It was a beach bag.

It was blue.

It was blank.

It was bumpy.

It was boring.

It was Oliver's beach bag.

"My beach bag!" Oliver cried.

"What is it doing *here*?"

"It was *always* here," I said.

"No one took it.

But someone took your *beach ball*.

Someone picked it up and threw it.

Or kicked it. Or carried it.

And I think it got thrown or kicked

again and again.

It landed a long way

from where you left it.

The sand was not pressed down

next to where you found

your beach ball

because your beach bag

had never been there.

But Annie gave me the big clue.

She and Fang are running

from one end of the beach

to the other.

I saw them run

toward the place

where you said you had left

your beach bag and ball.

But she had already *seen*

your ball and bag.

How could she see them

when she had not yet reached the place

where you said you had left them?

She or you had to be wrong."

"So you picked me?" Oliver asked.

"Yes, I, Nate the Great, picked you.

After someone almost hit me

on the head

with a beach ball.

That is when I thought

that the ball, not the bag,

had moved.

You left your beach bag

and beach ball *here*.

You went to Rosamond's Restaurant

over there. Then what did you do?"

"I drank my glass of water

and followed Esmeralda," Oliver said.

"When I saw my beach ball, I stopped."

"I, Nate the Great, say that

you followed Esmeralda *away* from

where you left your bag and ball.

When you saw your ball

you thought you were back
at where you had left it.
It is easy to get mixed up
on the beach.
If you are following someone,
it is even easier.
The case is solved."
"I will never follow anyone
again," Oliver said.

"Good," I said. "Sludge and I
are going for a swim."
"I just changed my mind,"
Oliver said.
"I knew it," I said.
I, Nate the Great,
and Sludge,
and Oliver, of course,
dove into the water.

~Extra~
Fun Activities!

What's Inside

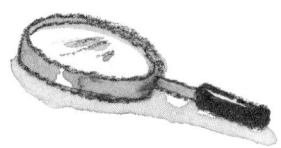

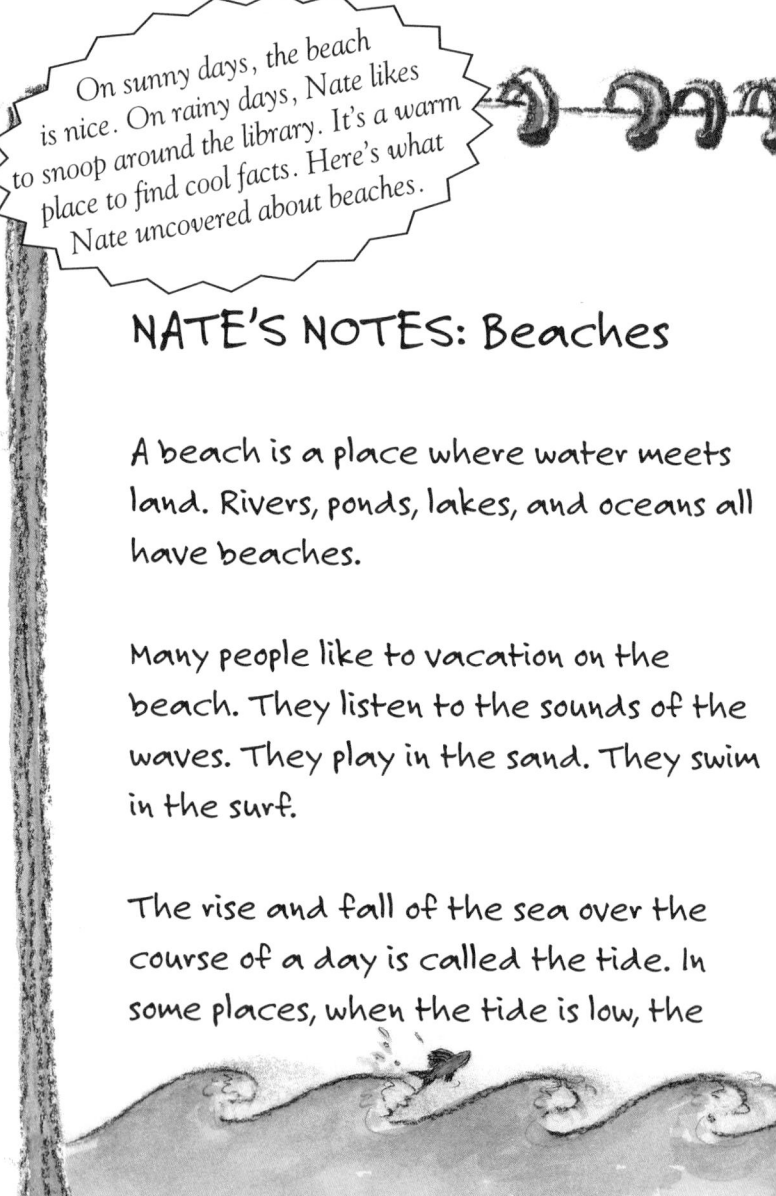

On sunny days, the beach is nice. On rainy days, Nate likes to snoop around the library. It's a warm place to find cool facts. Here's what Nate uncovered about beaches.

NATE'S NOTES: Beaches

A beach is a place where water meets land. Rivers, ponds, lakes, and oceans all have beaches.

Many people like to vacation on the beach. They listen to the sounds of the waves. They play in the sand. They swim in the surf.

The rise and fall of the sea over the course of a day is called the tide. In some places, when the tide is low, the

sea goes out so far from the beach that you can hardly see the water. At high tide, a boat in a harbor may bob on the waves. At low tide, the same boat may be stuck in the mud.

What creates the tide? Two things. One is the moon. When the moon is overhead, it pulls the water under it on Earth into a bulge. The second thing is Earth's rotation, or spin. Earth's spin makes the ocean water bulge out on the side away from the moon. These two bulges travel around Earth, creating two high tides on the planet every twenty-four hours and fifty minutes. That's how long the moon takes to circle Earth.

Beach sand comes from rocks, shells, and the bones of sea animals. Wind and water slowly grind this stuff into tiny pieces.

Different beaches have different types of sand. In Hawaii, rock from volcanoes makes black sand. In Bermuda, tiny red-shelled sea creatures called foram become pink sand. Hills of red sandstone turn into red sand in Jordan (a country in the Middle East).

Sand is the main ingredient in glass.

Jordan

Bermuda

Hawaii

Earthquakes, landslides, and volcanoes can create huge waves. They are called tsunami (soo-NAH-mee). Tsunami race across the ocean as fast as 500 miles per hour. The waves can be as tall as twenty people. They can wipe out buildings on shore. They can kill people. Luckily, tsunami are rare!

NATE'S NOTES: Beach Critters

Many animals live in the sand. Others live in the shallow water near the beach. Here are some critters you might see at the beach.

BARNACLES live on beaches that are underwater only at high tide. Barnacles make a glue that lets them stick themselves to smooth surfaces, like wooden piers. When water covers them, they suck in tiny bits of food. They like to eat wee plants, small clams, and other tiny stuff.

Barnacles

CRABS have a hard shell and ten legs. If they lose a leg, they grow it back! Crabs walk sideways. Some crabs can breathe both underwater and on land. They use their big claws to dig, tear food, and fight. They also move their claws to speak "sign language" with other crabs.

WHELKS are snails that live on the seashore.

HERMIT CRABS don't have hard shells, as other crabs do. They live in the shells of animals, such as whelks, that have died. As they grow, they move into bigger shells.

Hermit Crab "Home"

Lightning Whelk

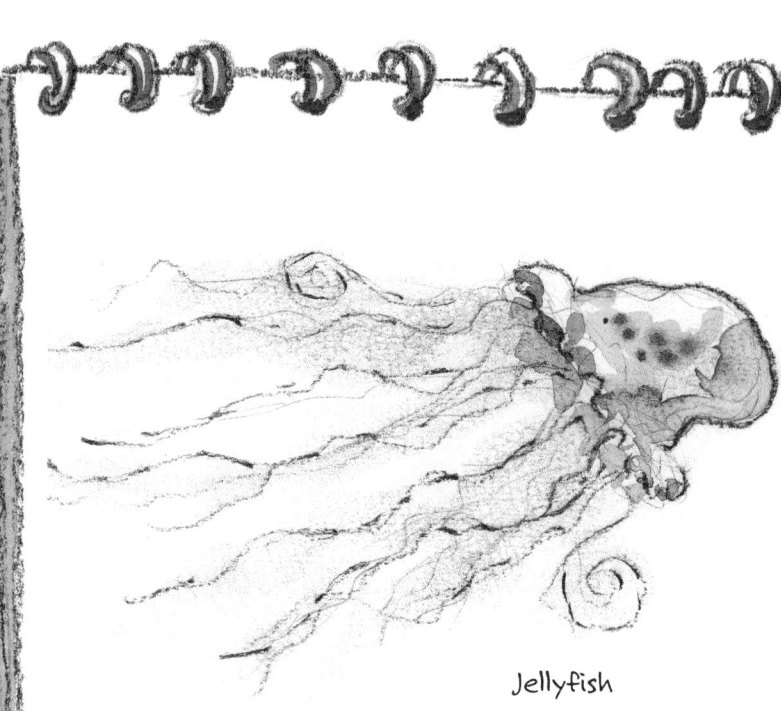

Jellyfish

JELLYFISH look like small parachutes floating in the water. Don't swim near them! Many jellyfish have tentacles, which they use to sting fish they want to eat. If they think you're a fish, you can end up with a painful, itchy rash.

SAND FLIES are so small that some people call them no-see-ums, but they pack a big bite. And, like mosquitoes, they suck human blood.

TURTLES like to live in shallow waters. Some also like to swim in the open sea. People sometimes find loggerhead turtles three thousand miles from the beach where they were born.

Some FISH, such as LOOKDOWNS, live in shallow water. These silver fish swim in schools of as many as five hundred. They get their name from their stuck-up expression.

Lookdowns

1

SEAGULLS can drink salt water. Special tubes in their heads clean out the salt. They will also eat almost anything. Some gulls even eat plastic. That can kill them! This is one good reason to keep the beach clean.

STARFISH are weird. They have no heads! They also have no backs or fronts. They hold on to rocks with tiny suction-cup feet. Most starfish have five arms, but one kind has twenty. If cut in half, some starfish can grow into two healthy animals.

Eight Fun Things to Do on the Beach

1. Swim. Use the buddy system. (Nate always swims with Oliver—whether Nate likes it or not.)

2. Build a sand castle. Use a bucket and wet sand to form walls, towers, and bridges. Or scoop up a handful of soaking wet sand and let it dribble from your fingers to create a drip castle.

3. **Play tic-tac-toe** in the sand.

4. **Gaze at the clouds.** Which one is the most mysterious? Which one looks most like a pancake?

5. **Fly a kite.** (See pages 21 to 24.)

6. Have a relay race. Draw a line in the sand. Walk 100 paces. Draw another line. Divide your friends into teams. Have the teams line up behind the first line. Yell "Ready, set— go!" On "go," each of the first runners runs to the second line, turns around, runs back, and tags the next member of the team. Keep going until everyone has run. Try having team members pass beach balls. Or try crab-walking!

7. Do the long jump. Draw a line in the sand. Stand behind the line and see how far you can jump. Can you jump farther with a running start?

8. Go on a treasure hunt. (See pages 16 to 20.)

How to Have a
Beach Treasure Hunt

Nate finds Oliver's bag on the beach. What can you find?

GET TOGETHER:

- this list
- a shovel to help you dig
- a pail to hold your treasures
- paper
- something to write with
- a camera, if you have one

Sand—Scoop a shovelful of sand into your pail. Examine it. What color are the tiny pieces? Are all the pieces the same shape? Are they all the same size?

Shells—On some beaches, it's hard to find even one shell. Other beaches are covered with shells. If your beach is covered with shells, find three with different shapes.

Driftwood—Waves and sand smooth the edges of driftwood. Salt turns it white. If your piece of driftwood is small, put it in your pail. If you find a big piece, take a picture. Or write a sentence about it on your paper.

A beach critter—Can you find a whelk or a hermit crab? How about a barnacle or a starfish? Watch your critter. Touch it gently. Leave it where you found it.

Seaweed—Lots of plants grow in oceans or lakes. They can be green, yellow, or brown. Some have bubbles, or pockets of air, that help them float. Some are slimy. Put a piece of seaweed in your pail. Or draw a picture of what you find.

Shorebirds—Pigeons and seagulls make their homes on city beaches. Big-billed pelicans live in Florida, California, and the Carolinas. Ducks and geese like lakes everywhere. See if you can spot three different kinds of birds. Write a sentence to describe each one.

People—Can you count the people sharing your beach? Or is it too crowded?

Trash—Pick up one piece of paper or plastic that doesn't belong on the beach. When you leave, put it in the trash.

Fish—Look for tiny fish in pools of seawater left behind at low tide, schools of fish in shallow surf, or fish bones on the sand.

Something left by people fishing—Can you find an old hook or bobber? How about a piece of net or trap? Don't pick up anything that looks rusty or sharp!

Something else you find!

How to Make a Kite

Beaches are usually windy. That makes them great places to fly a kite.

Ask an adult to help you with this project.

GET TOGETHER:

- a piece of $8^1/2$-by-11-inch paper
- a roll of masking tape
- an 8-inch bamboo stick
  (used to make shish kebabs)*
- a hole punch
- a ball of string
- scissors
- a roll of plastic surveyor's tape**

* Look for shish kebab sticks at the supermarket.

** You can buy surveyor's tape at a hardware store.

MAKE YOUR KITE:

1. Fold the paper in half so that it measures
   $8^1/_2$ by $5^1/_2$ inches.

2. Put the folded edge on the left.

3. Fold the right side over diagonally.

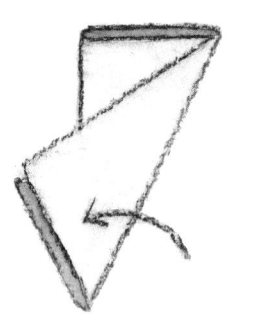

4. Open the diagonal fold. Use the masking tape to seal the crease completely.

5. Tape the bamboo stick across the paper as shown in the diagram.

6. Flip your kite over. Fold the front flap back and forth until it stands straight up.

7. Punch a hole in the flap about 1/3 of the way down from the pointy front end of the kite.
8. Tie the loose end of the ball of string to the hole.
9. Cut a piece of surveyor's tape about three feet long. Tape it to the front of the kite near the bottom. This is your kite's tail.
10. Go fly a kite!

How to Make Ocean Ice Pops

Playing on the beach can make you hot and thirsty. Cool off with these cool blue pops.

Makes six pops.

GET TOGETHER:

- fish-shaped candies
- 6 Dixie cups or other paper cups
- blue Gatorade (or another blue sports drink)
- 6 craft sticks*

*You can find these at a supermarket or a big variety store.

MAKE YOUR POPS:

1. Plop one or two candy fish into each cup.
2. Fill each cup 2/3 full of sports drink.
3. Place the cups in the freezer. Wait 60 minutes, then add a craft stick to each cup.
4. Leave the cups in the freezer at least four more hours.
5. Take out the pops. Peel off the paper cups.
6. Slurp up your pops! Share with your friends.

How to Make
Starfish Sandwiches

Rosamond sells sand sandwiches. If you're hungry, these taste better.

Makes about a dozen large or two dozen small sandwiches.

GET TOGETHER:

- a loaf of bread sliced very thin (Pepperidge Farm Very Thin works great.)
- mayonnaise
- a pound of sliced American cheese
- a star-shaped cookie cutter

MAKE YOUR SANDWICHES:

1. Lay one slice of bread on a clean, flat surface. Spread with mayonnaise.
2. Put a slice of cheese on the bread.
3. Place another slice of bread on top of the cheese.
4. Use the cookie cutter to cut star shapes. Get as many stars as you can out of each sandwich. (Save the scraps to eat later, if you wish.)

A word about learning with

Nate the Great

The Nate the Great series is good fun and has been entertaining children for over forty years. These books are also valuable learning tools in and out of the classroom.

Nate's world—his home, his friends, his neighborhood—is one that every young person recognizes. Nate introduces beginning readers and those who have graduated to early chapter books to the detective mystery genre, and they respond to Nate's commitment to solving the case and helping his friends.

What's more, as Nate the Great solves his cases, readers learn with him. Nate unravels mysteries by using evidence collection, cogent reasoning, problem-solving, analytical skills, and logic in a way that teaches readers to develop critical-thinking abilities. The stories help children start discussions about how to approach difficult situations and give them tools to resolve them.

When you read a Nate the Great book with a child, or when a child reads a Nate the Great mystery on his or her own, the child is guaranteed a satisfying ending that will have taught him or her important classroom and life skills. We know that you and your children will enjoy reading and learning from Nate the Great's wonderful stories as much as we do.

Find out more at NatetheGreatBooks.com.

Happy reading and learning with Nate!

Solve all the mysteries with

Nate the Great